OutLawed!

Tales of crime and adventure

Compiled by Wendy Body and Pat Edwards

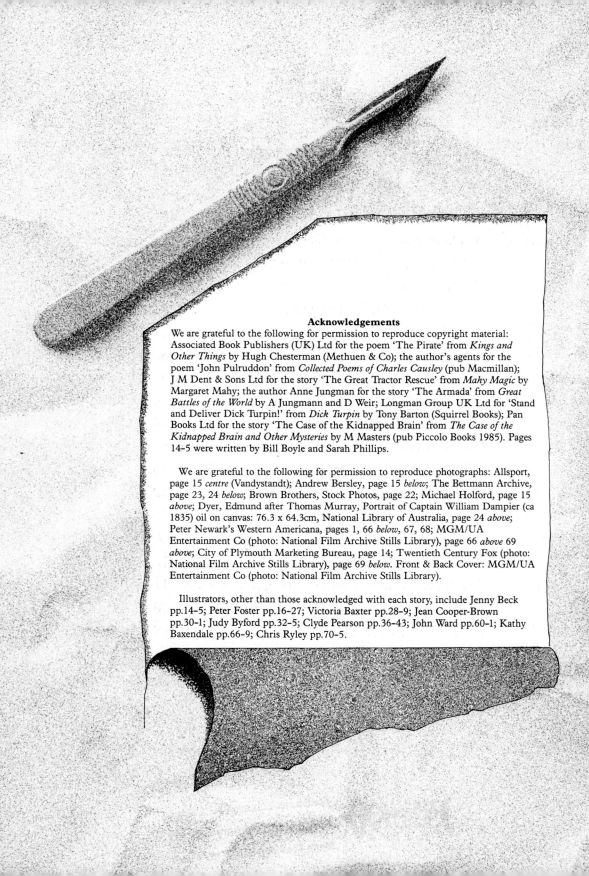

Acknowledgements

We are grateful to the following for permission to reproduce copyright material: Associated Book Publishers (UK) Ltd for the poem 'The Pirate' from *Kings and Other Things* by Hugh Chesterman (Methuen & Co); the author's agents for the poem 'John Pulruddon' from *Collected Poems of Charles Causley* (pub Macmillan); J M Dent & Sons Ltd for the story 'The Great Tractor Rescue' from *Mahy Magic* by Margaret Mahy; the author Anne Jungman for the story 'The Armada' from *Great Battles of the World* by A Jungmann and D Weir; Longman Group UK Ltd for 'Stand and Deliver Dick Turpin!' from *Dick Turpin* by Tony Barton (Squirrel Books); Pan Books Ltd for the story 'The Case of the Kidnapped Brain' from *The Case of the Kidnapped Brain and Other Mysteries* by M Masters (pub Piccolo Books 1985). Pages 14-5 were written by Bill Boyle and Sarah Phillips.

We are grateful to the following for permission to reproduce photographs: Allsport, page 15 *centre* (Vandystandt); Andrew Bersley, page 15 *below*; The Bettmann Archive, page 23, 24 *below*; Brown Brothers, Stock Photos, page 22; Michael Holford, page 15 *above*; Dyer, Edmund after Thomas Murray, Portrait of Captain William Dampier (ca 1835) oil on canvas: 76.3 x 64.3cm, National Library of Australia, page 24 *above*; Peter Newark's Western Americana, pages 1, 66 *below*, 67, 68; MGM/UA Entertainment Co (photo: National Film Archive Stills Library), page 66 *above* 69 *above*; City of Plymouth Marketing Bureau, page 14; Twentieth Century Fox (photo: National Film Archive Stills Library), page 69 *below*. Front & Back Cover: MGM/UA Entertainment Co (photo: National Film Archive Stills Library).

Illustrators, other than those acknowledged with each story, include Jenny Beck pp.14-5; Peter Foster pp.16-27; Victoria Baxter pp.28-9; Jean Cooper-Brown pp.30-1; Judy Byford pp.32-5; Clyde Pearson pp.36-43; John Ward pp.60-1; Kathy Baxendale pp.66-9; Chris Ryley pp.70-5.

Contents

THIRTEEN BANDITS

An Italian folk-tale adapted by PAT EDWARDS, illustrated by PETER FOST[...]

One day, when a poor farmer was searching in the forest for his cow, he saw a strange sight.

Open Oak!

They look like bandits. I wonder what they're up to?

4

A door in the oak opened and the bandits filed inside.

Close Oak!

There were thirteen of them and they all fitted inside that tree. *AMAZING!*

Full of curiosity, the farmer waited until the bandits appeared again.

Close Oak!

When's the next job?

I must see inside that tree!

As soon as all thirteen bandits had left, the farmer went to the tree.

Open Oak!

Sure enough the door opened.

Steps! I wonder where they lead to?

Down the steps went the farmer.

How exciting!

Deep in the ground...

WOW!

The farmer could hardly believe his eyes.

TREASURE!!!

Quickly the farmer scooped up all he could carry.

Then he went slowly jingling home...

to surprise his wife.

Wait till you see what's inside!

PLONK!

?

6

We're rich!

I can't believe it!

I'll go and borrow my brother's measure so we can work out how many gold coins we have!

Don't tell him why we want it.

ut the farmer's brother, ho was a cobbler nd so had more oney than the rmer, was sus- cious. He put a sh hook in the ottom of the easure. Sure ough, when the easure came back...

A-ha! I thought he was up to something!

And the farmer was forced to tell his brother where the gold had come from.

So I hurried home with the treasure!

I can't wait to visit that tree.

he cobbler insisted on being led to the tree and being a greedy man ne took a donkey and three sacks.

Open Oak!

That night he went home a very rich man indeed.

My advice is never go near that tree again.

Don't worry! I'll never need to!

7

"Greedy villain! Prepare to DIE!"

And the next part of the story is so bloodthirsty, we cannot bear to show it. For you see the bandit swung his sword so strongly he cut the cobbler clean in half.

UGH!

Late that night the cobbler's wife begged her brother-in-law to search for her husband who had not returned home. The farmer went straight to the oak tree.

There in the bushes lay the two pieces of his brother.

"Alas, my foolish brother, how dearly you paid for your greed!"

"I cannot take him home like this for his wife and children to see."

"I know! I'll call first on the other cobbler. I'm sure he'll help!"

"So, do you think you can sew him back together again?"

"A nasty task, but I'll do it to save more pain for his family."

"Thank you, friend."

A Cobbler lies here. MAY HIS SOLE REST IN PEACE

After the funeral service the cobbler's widow closed the shoe shop and used the stolen gold to buy the local tavern. People were surprised by her sudden wealth, but she never told where it came from.

So the two bandits went inside the tavern while the others waited in the cask.

Now as it happened the widow's daughter came running past.

She dropped her ball and it rolled beneath the cart.

As she crawled to get it, she was astonished to hear voices from the cask.

11

She ran to tell her mother.

Mother! Mother! Listen!

There are men inside that cask and they are plotting to kill us.

Run and fetch your uncle from the market. *QUICKLY!*

I'll put this sleeping powder in the wine.

I brought you some wine to drink while the macaroni cooks!

Don't whistle yet. We might as well enjoy the wine first!

Two swallows... and they were sound asleep.

ZZZZZ Z

SNK!

SNORE!

12

The farmer came racing to the tavern.

Quick, Brother-in-law, there are bandits out in that cask!

It's my home
The West Country

I am Sir Francis Dr... I am a great sailor and sea captain fro... the West Country. I played a very important part in the defeat of the Armada.

From very early on Plymouth has been an important port and naval base.

In 1588 the Spaniards sent an Armada (fleet) to invade England. The British fleet sailed from Plymouth and defeated the Spanish fleet. The 400th anniversary of the victory was celebrated in July 1988.

The rocky coastline used to wreck many ships. Lighthouses were very important, but it was hard to build them strong enough to survive the storms. Smeaton's lighthouse, which was built in 1759 for the Eddystone rocks (off the coast at Plymouth), lasted for over a hundred years. It has now been rebuilt in Plymouth to remind people of those who worked so hard to provide a light for ships.

The West Country is a peninsu... with water on three sides of the land, so there are lots of little harbours. These harbours mad... fairly easy for people to smugg...

e West Country is full of legends. The best
own are about King Arthur and his knights. At
tagel in Cornwall you can visit the ruins of his
tle, and also the cave of Merlin, the magician.

> Have you tried clotted cream? It's thick, almost solid cream made from the rich milk in the West Country. Eat it on scones with jam!

ere are many fine surf beaches in Devon and Cornwall. Fistral
ach at Newquay is particularly good. The Surfing World
ampionships have quite often been held here.

e rocks at Land's End are England's most westerly point. People
ite often walk or cycle from here to John O'Groats in north east
otland to raise money for charity. Do you know how far it is?

15

PIRATES!

Pirate stories are great adventure stuff, aren't they? If you've read Robert Louis Stevenson's *Treasure Island* you'll know all about the dastardly plotting that goes on whenever a gang of pirates gets together. You'll know about treasure buried in a secret place, about poor sailors walking the plank. You'll know all about the storybook pirates ...

Ship ahoy, Cap'n. Ship ahoy!

A treasure ship! Let's close in.

Are you ready on the guns, lads?

Aye, Aye Cap'n.

Cutlasses ready?

Aye, Aye, Cap'n!

Down with the flag! Up with the *Jolly Roger!*

She's trying to escape from us!

She can't escape. FIRE!

Exciting reading? Yes, but the storybooks only concentrate on the adventure, not on the horrible crimes committed.

Now meet the real pirates...

There were pirates long before the invention of writing. There were Greek pirates, Roman pirates, Viking pirates, Chinese pirates, Moslem pirates, long before there were English and other European pirates. Most of them were heartless. They attacked other ships, sinking them and sailing off to leave only bodies floating in the sea. Or they attacked quiet towns, plundering them and turning homes and storehouses into burnt-out ruins.

Even today, pirates sail the seas. In the Indian Ocean especially, they have attacked defenceless refugee ships from Vietnam.

1. Caribbean Sea
2. English Channel
3. Straits of Gibraltar
4. Strait of Messina
5. Mozambique Channel
6. Red Sea
7. Palk Strait
8. Malacca Straits
9. Formosa Strait
10. Korea Strait

A world of pirates

The seas are wide and lonely, and 400 years ago they were not very safe. Sooner or later ships must come to port, often having to sail through narrow straits and entrances. It was in places like these that pirates lurked, waiting to pounce on luckless cargo vessels. This Map shows some of the best places (from the pirate's point of view).

The Caribbean

Christopher Columbus sailed west across the Atlantic Ocean in 1492. He was seeking a way by sea to the "Indies", the rich lands of India and Cathay (as China was called). Instead, he found the Caribbean Islands.

Columbus was working for Queen Isabella of Spain, so in 1493, completely ignoring the people who lived in them, Pope Alexander VI declared that Spain now owned all the land to the west of the Caribbean. "Other people keep out!" in other words. All the treasures of this "New World" were to belong to Spain. And there was certainly treasure, especially gold. Before long, a rich trade sprang up and only the Spanish were allowed to buy and sell goods there.

The French, the English and the Dutch watched angrily. They wanted a share too, but Spain was rich and powerful at this time — much too powerful for them to risk going to war with her.

There were other ways, though, for these countries to get their hands on that treasure. They decided to let it be known that they wouldn't punish any of their sea captains who attacked homeward-bound Spanish ships — providing the captains first asked permission from their own country and providing they handed over to it most of the treasure.

The captains were only too delighted, especially when they were called "privateers" — pirate ship owners who had a licence to attack Spanish ships. It sounded better than "pirates" — much better!

GOLD FROM PANAMA!

For nearly two hundred years, the Spanish built their empire in Central America and South America. Richest of all the cities was Panama, for all the treasure (from Mexico in the north to Chile in the south) poured into it. From Panama, the treasure was carried by mule train over the mountains and down through the thick forests of the isthmus to Nombre de Dios. From there, heavily armed fleets of ships carried the rich cargo off to Spain.

In 1572 the English privateer, Francis Drake, attacked Nombre de Dios, expecting to capture a shipment of gold. But he was too late. It was already on the high seas. Refusing to give up, Drake and his men marched inland and ambushed the next mule train. Triumphantly, they sailed back to England with a hold full of around 100 000 gold doubloons. Drake's reward? The very grateful Queen Elizabeth pocketed her share of all he took and made him Sir Francis!

There are four names for these robbers of the high seas:

1 privateers: as you now know, these were seamen who were
   encouraged by their governments to prey on ships
   belonging to other countries.

2 pirates: a word which comes from the Latin word *pirata*
   which means one who robs or plunders on the sea.

3 buccaneers: robbers who lived in the seventeenth and
   eighteenth centuries and robbed only Spanish ships and
   American colonies.

4 corsairs: these were usually North African pirates who
   plundered the coast of Spain for treasure and slaves. This
   word comes from the French *corsaire* meaning "pirate".

Famous Privateers and Pirates

Captain John Avery, alias Long Ben
Born in Devon, England in 1665. Was elected pirate captain after the ship's crew mutinied. Sailed the seas off the West Indies and West Africa, and in the Red Sea. Took booty from the ship of the Great Mogul (Emperor of Delhi) — including 100 000 pieces of eight and the Mogul's daughter. Eventually died in poverty back in Devon.

Captain Hiram Breakes
A Dutch pirate from the island of Saba, West Indies. Sailed in both the Atlantic and the Mediterranean. Always described as a bloodthirsty cut-throat, he retired to Holland as a very rich man, but became depressed and killed himself.

Captain William Kidd
Said to have been born in Scotland about 1645. Nothing is known of his

CAPT KIDD

early years at sea, but by 1690 William was a ship owner living in New York. Five years later he was asked to help get rid of the pirates in the Indian Ocean. He was also told the English government would be quite happy if he seized any French ships he came across. Off sailed William to Madagascar and the east coast of Africa where, once he had the chance to sample the life, he switched sides and set about happily plundering the English ships he'd been sent to protect.

It was to be a very short career, however. In 1699 he was arrested in the West Indies and on 23 May 1701, the notorious Captain Kidd was hanged in London. Nearly 300 years later people are still hunting for his treasure which many believe is still buried somewhere on Long Island, New York.

John Rackham, nicknamed Calico Jack

Born in Jamaica. West Indies. A dashing pirate who took many prizes. Married Ann Bonney, also a pirate. She wore men's clothes and fought alongside Calico Jack. But the British Navy caught their ship in the West Indies. In 1720, Calico Jack was hanged and Ann Bonney was sent to prison.

Captain Edward Teach, nicknamed Blackbeard

Probably born in Bristol, England. Turned pirate in the West Indies in 1716 and for a time terrified the American province of Carolina. To make himself look ferocious, he used to wear two slow-burning matches beneath the brim of his hat! He was killed in 1718.

Blackbeard

Captain William Dampier

Born in Somerset, England around 1651. Joined a group of buccaneers in 1685 and eventually reached north-west Australia in 1688. Returned to England and later published a book titled *A New Voyage Round the World*. This so impressed the British government, they promptly made William a naval captain and in 1699 sent him out to explore the unknown coasts of New Holland (as Australia was then known) and New Guinea. His naval career wasn't a success. Eventually he went back to pirating and joined a privateer to plunder Spanish ships and Spanish towns on the west coast of South America. He died in 1715.

Sir Henry Morgan

Born in Wales around 1635. Kidnapped as a young boy in Bristol, he was sold as a servant in Barbados. He became a fearless buccaneer and at one time seized the whole of Spanish Panama, including Panama City where he took enormous treasure. For a time after this he was Lieutenant-Governor of Jamaica, but lost the job because he was too lenient with privateers and buccaneers. He died in 1688.

24

I do swear!

If you were a sailor whose ship was captured by pirates, you would be asked to join them. If you agreed, then you had to sign a copy of the ship's articles or rules. Here's a sample of what they were like:

> And you had to put your hand on either a Bible or a hatchet while you swore to obey them.

1. Every man shall obey Civil Command. The Captain shall have one full share and a half of all full prizes.

2. If any man shall offer to run away, or keep any secret from the Company, he shall be marooned with one Bottle of Powder, one Bottle of Water, one small Arm and Shot.

3. If any man shall steal anything in the Company, or gain, to the value of a Piece of Eight, he shall be marooned or shot.

4. That Man who shall strike another whilst these Articles are in force, shall receive Moses Law. (That is 40 stripes lacking 1 on the bare back.)

5. That man that shall snap his Arms, or smoke Tobacco in the Hold, without a Cap to his pipe, or carry a Candle lighted without a Lantern shall suffer the same punishment as in the former Article.

6. That Man that shall not keep his Arms clean, fit for an Engagement, or neglect his Business, shall be cut off from his share and suffer such other Punishment as the Captain and the Company shall think fit.

7. If any Man shall lose a Joint in time of an Engagement he shall have 400 Pieces of Eight; if a limb, 800.

8. If at any time you meet with a prudent Woman that Man that offers to meddle with her without her consent shall suffer present Death.

> A piece of eight was Spanish silver coin.

25

OTHER FASCINATING FACTS ABOUT PIRATES

Yo ho ho and a...

Although the most popular pirate flag showed a skull and crossbones, some crews flew a huge banner showing a skeleton holding a glass of punch.

There is no record anywhere of a man ever being made to walk the plank by pirates.

A very successful pirate named Captain Bartholomew Roberts drank only tea and allowed no gambling or women on board his ship. He stayed a captain for three years — a record for pirates!

Did you know the Pirate's flag is called 'The Jolly Roger'?

The Barbarossa brothers were two famous corsairs who ruled much of the Mediterranean from around 1515 until 1535. Great pirates and murderers, they collected huge fortunes and were heroes of Islam because they killed or enslaved Christians.

In 1702, William Dampier was a privateer in command of the *St George*. His companion ship was the *Cinque Ports* ("five ports"). It was the commander of *Cinque Ports* who marooned Alexander Selkirk on one of the islands in the Juan Fernandez group in the south-east Pacific. Later Daniel Defoe used Selkirk's adventures in his book *Robinson Crusoe*.

Cu te

Truth strang than fict

One not-so-successful pirate was Captain England. His crew decided he was too soft-hearted so they dumped him ashore on the island of Mauritius.

There were pirates in Greek waters up till 1850 and there are still pirates operating around Korea, China and Japan to this day. Before World War II, Chinese pirates often signed on as passengers, then later took over the ship and held it and everyone on board to ransom.

Fift men o dead che = Ph

Buccaneer, Captain Bartholomew Sharpe captured a Spanish man-of-war, then by accident threw overboard silver worth 150 000 pounds.

First of all the buccaneers was Frenchman Pierre Le Grand. One night he set out in an open boat with a crew of 28. He seized a Spanish galleon which he promptly sold in France, then retired to a life of ease.

Saddest story I ever heard!

Just like hijacking a plane!

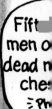

The Pirate

He walks the deck with swaggering gait,
(There's mischief in his eye)
Pedigree Pirate through and through,
With pistols, dirk and cutlass too;
A rollicking rip with scars to show
For every ship he's sent below.
His tongue is quick, his temper high,
And whenever he speaks they shout, "Ay, Ay!"
To this king of a roaring crew.

His ship's as old as the sea herself,
And foggity foul is she:
But what cares he for foul or fine?
If guns don't glitter and decks don't shine?
For sailormen from East to West
Have walked the plank at his request;
But if he's caught you may depend
He'll dangle high at the business end
Of a tickly, tarry line.

Hugh Chesterman

27

A computer story! Kate Francis

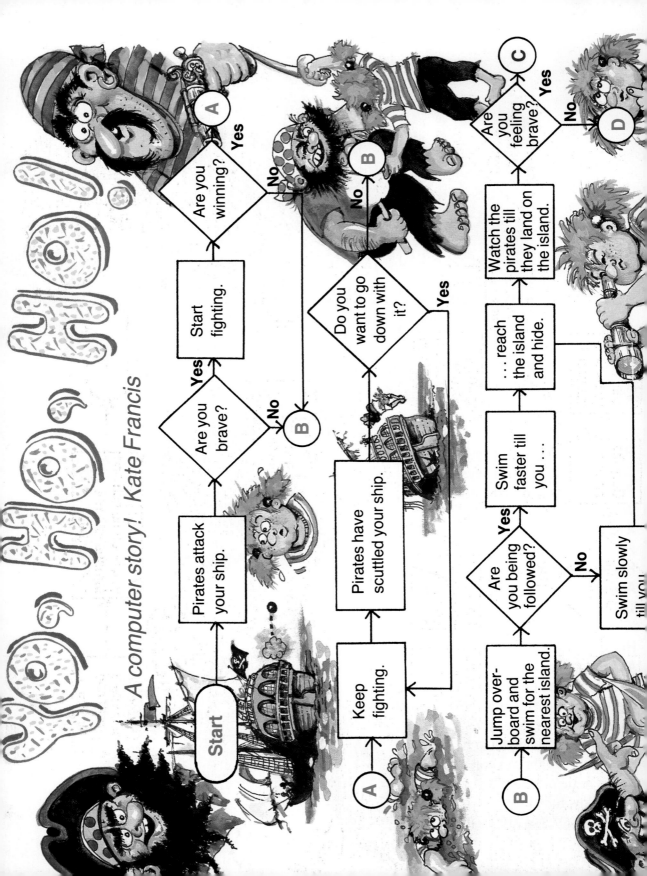

Start → Pirates attack your ship. → Are you brave? — **Yes** → Start fighting. → Are you winning? — **Yes** → (A)

Are you brave? — **No** → (B)

Are you winning? — **No** → (B)

(A) → Keep fighting. → Pirates have scuttled your ship. → Do you want to go down with it? — **Yes** → Jump overboard and swim for the nearest island.

Do you want to go down with it? — **No** → (B)

(B) → Jump overboard and swim for the nearest island. → Are you being followed? — **Yes** → Swim faster till you . . . → . . . reach the island and hide. → Watch the pirates till they land on the island. → Are you feeling brave? — **Yes** → (C)

Are you being followed? — **No** → Swim slowly till you . . .

Are you feeling brave? — **No** → (D)

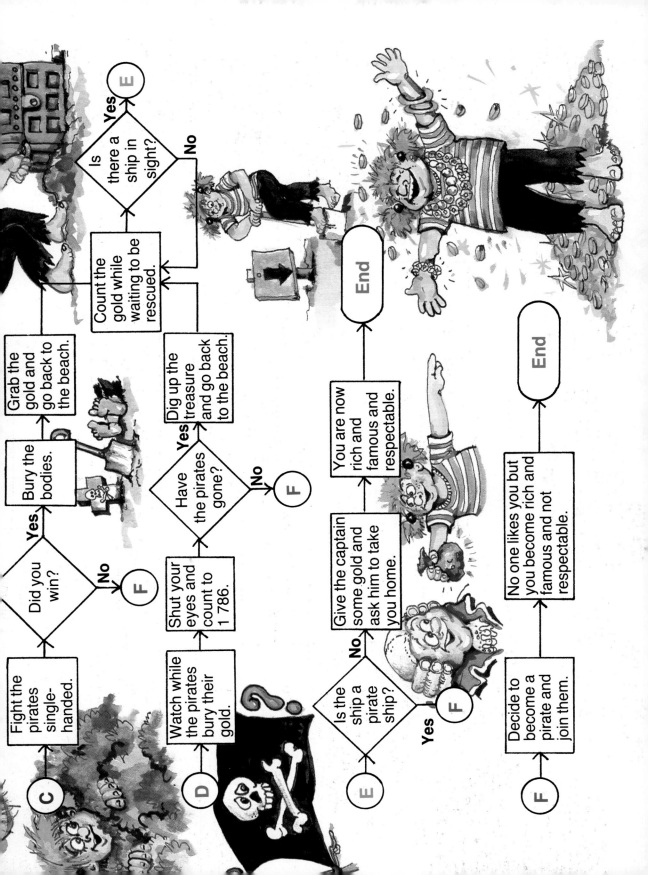

FAMOUS FEMALE PIRATES

People assume that only men were pirates, but in fact many women have been pirates and have been just as famous and fierce as the men. One Chinese woman who was a pirate commanded a fleet of almost two thousand junks (beautiful wooden sailing ships), crewed by men and women. Ching Yih Saou prowled the China Sea during the nineteenth century.

Ann Bonney and Mary Read were two pirating friends who came to a sticky end in 1720. Ann, the daughter of an American lawyer, sailed off to sea with Calico Jack. He was already notorious for his pirating escapades, and on one of their adventures together they captured the ship Mary Read was aboard. (Mary Read had been born and brought up in London and, dressed as a boy, had then run away to sea.) Mary joined them. However, some time later they were captured and the two women were imprisoned, where Mary died of fever.

A very unusual pirating story comes from England. Poor Sir John Killigrew must have been most embarrassed. During the 1850s his job was to try and stop piracy around England's coast. However, both his mother and his wife were pirates and it was said that no vessel was safe from their attack!

Yo ho ho! And a bottle of rum!

Australia had its share of women pirates. Charlotte Badger, 'one of the best pick-pockets in London', met fellow-convict Mary Barnes, on the long sea voyage out to New South Wales in the early 1800s. Not long after their arrival in Sydney, Charlotte hatched a daring plan. Both she and Mary were assigned as convict servants in Hobart Town. They boarded the *Venus* along with a gang of male convicts to make the journey to Tasmania. During the voyage, with the help of a couple of crew, Charlotte had all the firearms seized, and took command. The captain and most of his crew were set adrift in the ship's boat. After raiding another ship on the high seas, Charlotte and Mary eventually reached New Zealand. Mary became the wife of a Maori chieftain and, many years later, the skipper of an American whaling ship found Charlotte on a Tongan Island.

John Polruddon

John Polruddon
All of a sudden
Went out of his house one night,

When a privateer
Came sailing near
Under his window-light.

They saw his jugs
His plates and mugs
His hearth as bright as brass,

His gews and gaws
And kicks and shaws
All through their spying-glass.

They saw his wine
His silver shine
They heard his fiddlers play.

"Tonight," they said,
"Out of his bed
Polruddon we'll take away."

And from a skiff
They climbed the cliff
And crossed the salt-wet lawn,

And as they crept
Polruddon slept
The night away to dawn.

"In air or ground
What is that sound?"
Polruddon said, and stirred.

They breathed, "Be still,
It was the shrill
Of the scritch-owl you heard."

"O yet again
I hear it plain,
But do I wake or dream?

"In morning's fog
The otter-dog
Is whistling by the stream.

"Now from the sea
What comes for me
Beneath my window dark?"

"Lie still, my dear,
All that you hear
Is the red fox's bark,"

Swift from his bed
Polruddon was sped
Before the day was white,

And head and feet
Wrapped in a sheet
They bore him down the height.

And never more
Through his own door
Polruddon went nor came,

Though many a tide
Has turned beside
The cliff that bears his name.

On stone and brick
Was ivy thick;
And the grey roof was thin,

And winter's gale
With fists of hail
Broke all the windows in.

The chimney-crown
It tumbled down
And up grew the green,

Till on the cliff
It was as if
A house had never been.

But when the moon
Swims late or soon
Across St Austell Bay,

What sight, what sound
Haunts air and ground
Where once Polruddon lay?

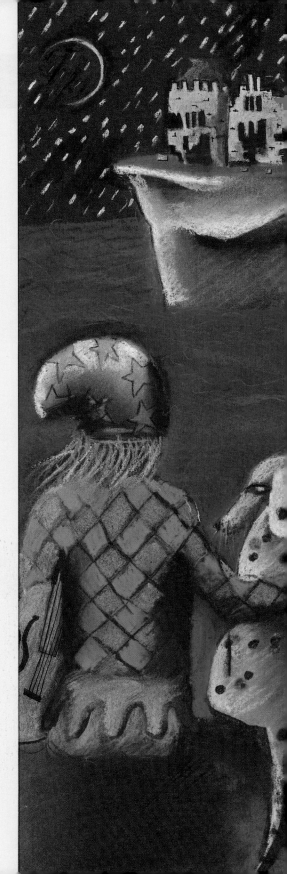

It is the high
White scritch-owl's cry,
The fox as dark as blood,

And on the hill
The otter still
Whistles beside the flood.

Charles Causley

(John Polruddon's house was on the cliff over
Pentewan, in south Cornwall. The story of his
disappearance dates from early Tudor times.)

The Armada

King Philip of Spain was the richest man in the world.
Every year ships full of treasure from the New World sailed
into his ports. But one day a messenger brought Philip bad
news.

"Your majesty, English ships have captured your
treasure and taken it to Queen Elizabeth."

Philip and his advisers were furious.

"Go to war!" they cried. "You can't let a woman take
your treasure."

"The English help our enemies!"

"They are not Catholics!"

"All right," agreed the King. "I'll teach Elizabeth and
the English a lesson. I shall send the greatest fleet of ships
ever seen against that miserable little island. I shall call this
fleet the 'Invincible Armada'." (unbeatable fleet)

At every port in Spain great ships called galleons were
built to carry thousands of men to crush England.

When Elizabeth heard about it, she was very worried.

"What shall we do?" she said. "My people are brave but
the Spanish are the greatest soldiers in the world."

"Don't worry," said Francis Drake, the most daring of
England's seamen. "Not one Spaniard will set foot on
English soil. We will sink their ships at sea."

"But how will I pay for the ships we need?" replied
Elizabeth. "And we need time."

"I shall destroy King Philip's ships," said Drake, "and
bring his treasure to you."

Medina Sidonia

So Francis Drake sailed right into the harbour of Cadiz where the ships of the Armada were moored and destroyed most of the eighty ships there. This was in 1587. Drake had made sure the Armada would not sail that year. On the way home Drake captured lots of treasure ships. When he got home, his ships were weighed down with treasure. People ran out of church to welcome him back.

The King of Spain was horrified when he learned that his ships were burned and his treasure stolen. However, Philip was determined not to make peace. He said,

"The Armada will sail next year. I appoint the Duke of Medina-Sidonia to organise it."

The Duke didn't want the job.

"I get sea-sick," he complained. "I'm not the right man at all."

But Philip insisted, so Medina-Sidonia organised the building of ships, finding crews, guns, cannons, food and wine. 30,000 men were to travel to England. Getting enough food and water was difficult.

Philip's plan was to send the Armada up the English Channel. There it would wipe out the English navy. Then the Armada would go to Holland to pick up the Spanish army fighting there.

Elizabeth used the time Drake had gained for her. She had as many ships built as possible.

On May 14th, 1588, the ships of the Armada finally sailed out of Lisbon harbour, cannons booming and thousands of men singing. However, from the beginning the Armada had only bad luck. The wind was wrong and they had to wait till June to sail north. Already the Armada was short of food, and men had to cover food with vinegar to kill the mouldy taste.

In England they waited for the Armada to appear. On July 29th they sighted the Spanish fleet off Cornwall. Messengers went immediately to Drake. He was busy playing bowls and decided to finish his game.

The Spaniards anchored near Plymouth. That night the English fleet sailed right past them, so close that they could hear Spanish voices. In the morning as light dawned the Spaniards were shocked to find that they were surrounded. In the fight that followed the fast-moving English ships did a lot of damage to the Spanish fleet and captured several ships. However, the Armada was still dangerous. Medina-Sidonia decided to go to France to get more guns and ammunition.

The English followed him to Calais. They had run out of cannon balls. They did not want to get close to the enemy, as then the Spanish soldiers would jump on board. So they built fire ships and set them alight. The crews of the fire ships jumped into small boats just before they crashed into the Spanish galleons. This time the Armada was finally defeated. Medina-Sidonia knew that the only thing he could do was go home as fast as possible. However, they could not sail along the English Channel, for the English were blocking it. So they sailed all the way round the north of Scotland and past Ireland. There were terrible storms, many ships were wrecked and men drowned. Others died of hunger and fever.

In September sixty-five ships out of one hundred and thirty returned to Spain. Only 3,000 men of the 30,000 survived. After that Elizabeth didn't worry about Spain. In the battle for the sea England with her fast light ships had won.

Robin hood and his merry men.

Travel long ago was hazardous: Pirates
at sea waiting to pounce on luckless ships,
and bandits on land, waiting to pounce on luckless
travellers. Australia had bushrangers, and England had
highwaymen and outlaws. Most were villains who roamed
the countryside, killing and stealing. But some were not,
or so the storybooks say!

Most famous of all storybook outlaws is Robin Hood. He is
believed to have lived in England in the 14th century. At that time,
England was ruled by the Normans who had sailed over from
France to invade England in 1066. The Normans drove the
Saxons (the people who had lived in England from the 5th or 6th
century) from their lands.

The Sheriff of Nottingham was a Norman and he ruled all the
land from Derby to Lincoln, including Sherwood Forest.
According to some stories, Robin Hood was the son of a Saxon
nobleman whose castle was burned by the Sheriff of Nottingham's
soldiers. Robin's father was captured and died in prison. Robin's
mother died soon afterwards. With no home, no parents, and no
money, Robin went to live in Sherwood Forest.

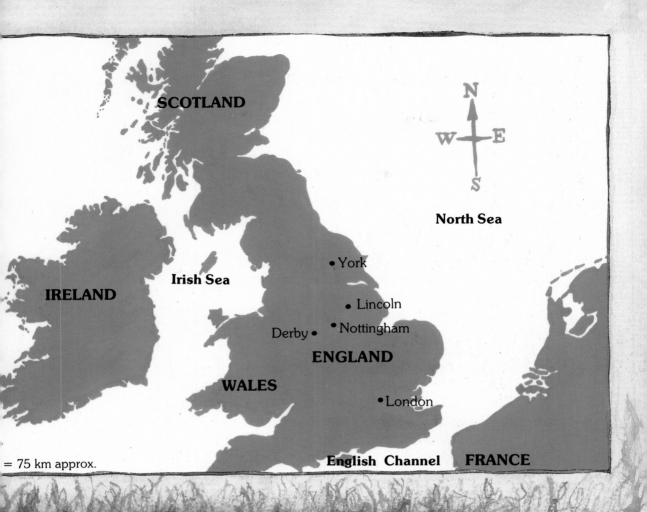

SCOTLAND

N
W E
S

North Sea

• York

Irish Sea

• Lincoln

IRELAND

Derby • • Nottingham

ENGLAND

WALES

• London

= 75 km approx.

English Channel　**FRANCE**

There were other Saxons living in Sherwood Forest. They were homeless men whose houses and land had been taken over by the Normans. Robin soon became their leader.

There were deer in the Forest so at least they had plenty to eat. But the Normans considered that the deer belonged to the King and they called Robin and his men "outlaws". If they caught an outlaw, the Normans killed him.

Robin and his men dressed themselves in Lincoln green and vowed to rob the rich and help the poor. Their fame spread and their numbers grew as others came to join them. Little John, Friar Tuck and Will Scarlet are three of the best known "Merry Men".

Little John

One morning Robin Hood said to his men, "We have not killed any deer for fourteen days. We must have food. Wait here and I'll go hunting. If I need help, I'll blow my horn."

So Robin went away with his bow and arrows, and he came to a stream with a bridge over it. It was a very narrow bridge and, as he started to cross, another man began to cross from the opposite side. He was over two metres tall and he carried a long staff in his hand. When they met in the middle, neither would give way.

"Good morning to you," said Robin. "Please stand back and let me pass."

The man stood there, and said nothing.

Robin put an arrow in his bow and began to move forward.

"You're afraid of me," said the man. "You have a bow and arrow and I have only a staff."

Robin put down his bow and arrow and said "We'll fight for the right to pass. The man who falls in the stream is the loser." Then he went and made a staff from a small tree.

So they fought on the bridge. They had been fighting for an hour when Robin hit the big man — *whack!* — on the head.

"Ha, ha!" Robin cried. "You nearly had a good wash that time!"

But he spoke too soon. The big man's staff came *bang* on the side of Robin's head and Robin fell into the water with a great splash.

The big man laughed, "Now who says 'ha, ha'? Have a good wash my friend!"

When Robin Hood climbed out of the stream, he was laughing too.

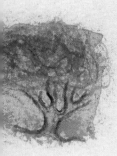

"You're a brave man," he said, "and you can hit hard". Robin felt the side of his head. "I lost, so what can I do for you?"

"Help me find Robin Hood," said the big man. "I want to be one of his men."

Robin Hood blew his horn. Very soon, twenty men in Lincoln green were at the bridge.

One said, "This man has thrown you into the stream, Robin. Let's throw him in too."

The big man said, "Robin? Robin? Are you Robin Hood? Did I hit Robin Hood with my staff?"

"Yes," said Robin, and he told the story to his men. They all laughed.

Then Robin Hood said to the big man, "I like you. Come with me and be one of my men. I'll give you a bow and arrows and teach you to shoot".

The man held out his hand. "Yes," he said, "I'll be one of your men".

Robin Hood said, "What's your name?"

"John Little," replied the man.

"Oh!" said Robin Hood. "We must change that. We'll call you Little John."

So Little John went with Robin Hood and his men. They killed two deer and roasted them over the fire, and they ate and drank till the sun went down.

Next morning Robin Hood gave Little John a coat of Lincoln green and a bow and arrows. He said, "Now I will teach you to shoot".

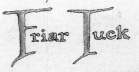 Friar Tuck

Little John could soon shoot very well. Because he was a very big man, they made a specially large bow for him. One day Robin Hood said to him, "Look at those deer on the hill far away. Shoot one of them".

Little John shot the deer.

Robin Hood was very pleased. He said, "I don't know anyone who can shoot better than that!"

Will Scarlet said, "I know someone who can. His name is Friar Tuck, and he can shoot better than you or Little John".

"I must find him!" cried Robin. "Where does he live?"

"He lives at Fountains Abbey," replied Will Scarlet.

Then Robin Hood put on a steel cap and he took a sword, and set off in search of Friar Tuck.

From the forest near Fountains Abbey, Robin Hood spotted Friar Tuck walking near a stream. He had a steel cap and a sword just like Robin Hood's steel cap and sword.

"Hide here," Robin Hood whispered to his men. Then he went out of the forest alone. He walked down to Friar Tuck and said, "Good morning, Friar. Please carry me over the stream".

Friar Tuck looked at Robin Hood. He saw a young man who could walk through the stream without help. But he knew that friars had to help other people and so he said, "Get on my back".

So Robin Hood got on Friar Tuck's back and Friar Tuck carried him over the stream.

"Thank you," Robin said, and he jumped down.

"Wait!" Friar Tuck said. "Have I helped you?"

"Yes."

"I'm glad," the Friar said. "I helped you because friars must help people. And now you can carry me back over the stream!" And he took out his sword.

So Robin Hood carried Friar Tuck back over the stream. The Friar was a big, fat man, and it was hard work. On the other side Robin caught Friar Tuck's hand and threw him — *thump!* — on the grass.

Now Robin took out his sword. "Carry me back again," he said, "or I'll kill you."

"All right! Get on my back."

Friar Tuck carried Robin Hood into the stream. Then — *splash*! — the big Friar tossed Robin into the water.

After that, the outlaws in the forest saw a great fight. The two swords were as quick as light. Friar Tuck's steel cap saved his head again and again, and more than once the Friar's sword fell *crash* on Robin Hood's cap.

At last Friar Tuck said, "I will not fight you any more. You're a very brave man. Who are you?"

"I am Robin Hood." He put his hand up, and the outlaws ran out of the forest. Robin said, "I came here to find a man who shoots very well with his bow and I have found a man who fights very well with a sword."

Will Scarlet said, "He shoots well, too. That man can shoot better than Little John or you, Robin."

Robin Hood said, "Now that I have found you, I ask you to come and join us. I and my men live in the forest. We take money from the rich and give it to the poor."

Friar Tuck said, "Friars must love God and help others. But I haven't done much good living here in this Abbey. So I will go with you."

And that was how Friar Tuck joined Robin Hood and his Merry Men.

Written by Michael West
Illustrated by Giovina Gaspari

51

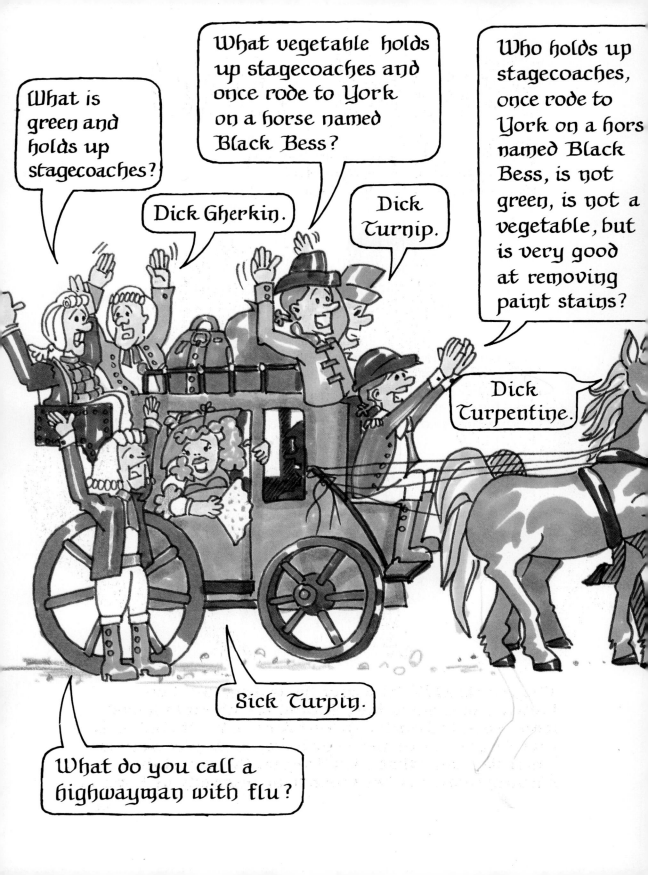

Stand and Deliver!

The year is 1737. The country is England. Peter
Fletcher and his father, Simon, are about to travel
from York to London to look for work. His father is
carrying all the money they have, so they're nervous
when they hear that Dick Turpin, the notorious
highwayman, has been seen near their city of York . . .

Peter and his father climbed up onto the top of the London coach. It was cheaper to ride "outside".

As they drove down the Great North Road, Peter had a lot of time to think about Dick Turpin. "Was it Turpin who tried to stop that coach yesterday? Will he stop us? Will he be kind to us?"

But for three days, the coach drove through forests and fields and cities, stopping many times. They stopped at the inns, to change horses, and they stopped at all the turnpike gates to pay the toll. A man waited at each turnpike to open the gate and collect the money.

Then, as they got near London, they came to the Green Man Inn in Epping Forest. The horses were tired and new horses would be waiting at the inn.

Peter was tired too. There was nothing to do on the coach. All the way he had been sitting next to a big fat man who talked and talked and made him sleepy. The man's name was Mr Buffard, and he never stopped talking about his farm and all the things that he did there. Peter looked at his father, and he knew from his face that he, too, thought the fat man talked too much.

Peter got down to see the inn and the things that were happening there. Two men were taking the tired horses away from the coach.

"Hey, Walter!" shouted the coachman to one of these men. "Give me some good horses now — I hear Turpin was in the forest last night."

Walter called back, "No, someone's been telling you lies, my friend. Turpin was at Blackheath last night. He stopped a man and took all his money and his horse. People say Turpin gave him back his watch, because the man said it was a present from his dear old mother."

The other man said, "But Walter, if he was in Blackheath last night, he could be in Epping tonight. His horse Black Bess is the quickest in England."

"All right, Joe," answered Walter, "but we must stop talking. Mr Bayes will be angry if we don't get on with our work!"

There were people everywhere at the inn. People talking, people laughing, people eating and drinking. Peter heard bells ringing inside the inn, shouts for more drinks, men and women running everywhere.

He sat down by a wall, and looked through all the legs moving so quickly. He saw a small, rat-faced boy in poor clothes like himself. The boy ran about looking at people all the time. He looked for a long time at Mr Buffard. The fat man was still talking but not to Simon Fletcher now.

At last, Walter and Joe came back with the horses. Soon, everyone got into their places in the coach.

Peter looked down and saw the poor boy again. Now he was speaking quickly to a man Peter had not seen before. The man looked at a gold watch in his hand, and there was more gold on his blue coat and his black hat. A beautiful black horse stood beside this man, her nose on his arm. He looked at the coach as it went out of the inn.

Peter thought, "He's looking at me. Or is it Mr Buffard? I'd like to know who he is. He looks rich."

The man said something to the rat-faced boy, got on his horse, and rode away.

The coachman drove the horses out onto the highway, and they were soon going along through the trees towards London. The light was not good in the forest. In some parts, the trees grew near the road. A man could hide in these places.

There had been no rain and
the road was good. All the
time the coachman drove his
horses hard. "I want to get
out of the forest soon," he said.

Peter thought about the
rat-faced boy, about working in
London, about a man in a blue
coat, with a black hat, and a
black horse. He was sleepy
again. But before he fell asleep
on Mr Buffard's arm, he heard
him say, "Mr Fletcher, a man
at the inn told me Turpin was
on Hounslow Heath last night,
stopping the Bristol coach.
If he tries to stop us . . . I'll . . ."
But he did not say what he
would do.

Peter wanted to know what
he was going to say, but he
couldn't make his eyes stay
open. He slept.

A shout woke him up, a
very big shout.

"Stand and deliver! Throw
down your money!"

Peter saw a black horse
standing on its back legs.
With one hand, the rider tried
to make it stand still. In his other
hand he had a pistol. His face
was covered with a cloth, but
Peter knew the blue coat at once.

There was no time to say anything. The horse was standing still now, and the pistol looked very big in the highwayman's hand. "Get out of the coach, all of you!" he shouted.

They all stood in the road.

"The first person who moves," he called out again, "I shall shoot him dead."

Peter stood very still, and took his father's hand.

The horseman spoke to Mr Buffard.

"You, sir," he said, "you look very fat. Lots to eat, sir? Lots of money, eh? How many yellow-boys have you got for me?"

Now Mr Buffard had nothing to say.

"Can't speak, sir?" said the highwayman with a laugh. "If you don't speak soon, my pop here will speak." His fingers moved on the pistol.

"Please, sir," said Mr Buffard, "I have no money."

"I've heard that story before," was the answer. The pistol moved towards the fat man's head.

Buffard called out at once. "Don't shoot! Don't shoot! Here's my money!" And he took out a bag and gave it to the highwayman.

"I thank you, sir," said the horseman, with another laugh. "You're very kind. Are there any more of you who would like to be kind?"

Unhappily, the people from the coach gave him their money. Two had watches; some of them had gold rings. Simon Fletcher took out his little bag of money, looked at it sadly, and then gave it to the highwayman. But Simon said nothing.

"Is *this* Dick Turpin?" Peter thought. "Dick Turpin doesn't take poor men's money!"

Without thinking, Peter shouted at him. "My father has worked very hard for that money! You can't take it from us!"

Everyone looked at Peter.

"We're not rich, we're poor!"

The highwayman looked down at the boy. "Poor, are you, boy? I'm poor too."

"No, you're not, you're rich! I saw you at the Green Man. I saw your gold watch. And that blue coat is new!"

The highwayman looked angry and said, "Do you want me to shoot you? You know what this is, don't you, boy?"

Simon Fletcher spoke at last. "You would not shoot a child?"

The eyes under the cloth on the man's face moved to look at Simon. The pistol came up towards his head. Peter put his arms round his father's legs.

Then the highwayman laughed. "No, sir, you speak well. I would not! Dick Turpin doesn't shoot children! Remember that, boy! Tell your friends you've spoken to Turpin and you're still alive!"

He kicked his horse's sides, shouted, "Come on, Bess!" and rode into the trees. As he went, he threw something onto the ground.

Peter ran and got it. "Look, Father! Your money!"

Mr Buffard was very angry. "Why didn't he give mine back?" His face got red all over. "I had twenty pounds in my bag. Quick, get the constables!"

Written by Tony Barton
Illustrated by David Bone

From Shank's Pony* to MOTOR COACH

* To travel by shank's pony means to

Up until the fifteenth century most people walked, carrying or dragging their goods.

Wheeled vehicles dated from around 8000 BC but were used only for agriculture, hunting or war. If you were rich, you got someone to carry you.

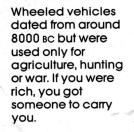

In the seventeenth century many countries, especially France, began to build roads. The English developed the 'long wagon'. It was covered, carried eight passengers who sat on the floor, and was pulled by six or more horses at around 5 kilometres per hour (kph). The French had the first city bus service in the world. It began in 1662, but was a failure.

1800s... More and better roads are built. Coaches now tear along at up to 15 kph.

Toll roads and turnpikes are built in many countries. Stage coaches become the way to travel from city to city.

1830s... The l[...] England says [...] man carrying [...] flag must wal[...] front of every s[...] carriage. Eng[...] begin to experiment w[...] internal comb[...] engine.

1769. Frenc[...] Nicholas C[...] built a stea[...] carriage.

60

But most people are still using horse-drawn coaches. (The poor still walk.)

1875 onwards. The first experimental cars are developed.

1900 onwards. The internal combustion engine takes over. The first cars do not have roofs or windows and hurtle along at up to 25 kph.

Motor buses appear as roads get better in all countries. Most people, however, still travel by train.

Today, motor coaches carry thousands of long-distance travellers by road. In many countries coaches are more popular than trains (and they're cheaper than planes!).

61

A WILD COLONIAL BOY.

Pages from Bridgit Malone's Diary

1 September, 1827

Today is my 10th Birthday and I, Bridgit Malone, have decided to keep a Diary so that when I am Old and Grey I will know what it was like to be 10 in the year 1827. 'Twas my Pa who gave me this notebook, telling me to practise my Letters in it, but I think I would rather keep it as a Diary. I will try to write in it Openly and Honestly and to record only those things that are Important and of Note.

22 September, 1827

Such excitement! Everyone is talking about the gang of Bushrangers that are Harrying our District. Today 3 farmers called in to talk about how we should all protect ourselves. I hid in the Geraniums by the side of the house and listened. As they were sitting out on the Verandah I could hear all they said. Mr O'Farrell did most of the talking. It seems the Leader of the Gang came out on the same ship as the convict who is working on his Farm. This man says that Jack Donahoe was a Wild One, always boasting that no one would lock him up behind iron bars. Well, of course they don't anyway. Most convicts work on Farms or on Road Gangs. Everyone knows that! Anyway, what Jack Donahoe did was persuade some other convicts to sneak off into the Bush and to hold up some Settlers who were coming Home from Market. But the Troopers came after them and they were all caught. The Judge sentenced them to be Hanged. (My Stomach turns over when I think of what it must be like to hear a Judge say solemnly that your life is to end). But Against All Odds, Jack Donahoe escaped again and now he is turned Bushranger. Ma asked where he came from and Mr O'Farrell said Dublin and Ma sighed and said, "At least there's one Mother who has more to grieve about than mine." Then the men started talking about sheep and I crept away. But Oh how my Head did buzz with all that news!

17 March, 1828

St. Patrick's Day and what a Gathering we had! And how tongues wagged about Bold Jack Donahoe. Some were calling him The Stripper. I'm not sure why. Perhaps because he strips his Victims of all they have. Half the People seemed to admire him for his Daring and half were angry because they said it meant the troopers gave all the Irish a bad time. Someone said the gang had held up the Reverend Samuel Marsden and Jack Donahoe threatened to kill him for hanging so many convicts. I heard Mr O'Farrell say not many would shed a tear for the Flogging Parson, but his wife told him not to talk so loud. Then Ma saw me listening and sent me off to help in the kitchen.

2 January, 1829

Yesterday we visited the O'Farrells and of course the talk turned to The Stripper and his Gang. For a whole year and 4 months now they have ranged the Country side. Everyone knows Someone who knows Something about this Bold Outlaw. Pa said he won't live to be much older, but I think he is too Clever to be caught.

1 September, 1829

Today is my Twelfth Birthday. Truly, I feel Older. Mr O'Farrell called in today. He said the town was buzzing with the latest about Jack Donahoe. Who did he hold up but Mr Charles Sturt, the explorer who only this year discovered that the Macquarie River flows into the Castlereagh! When The Stripper recognised his Victim he said, "I'll not rob a man whose Accomplishments I Respect," and forbade his men to take even a penny. How Romantic and Gallant he is, even though a Criminal.

28 March, 1830

'Tis now Two and one Half Years since I began keeping this Diary. That makes it Two and one Half Years since Jack Donahoe and his companions began their Wild Careers. Pa says their luck must run out soon. Ma cannot understand why no one has turned him in for the reward, but Pa holds that no matter how bad an Irishman is, another Irishman will never turn him over to English troopers. Ma said "Tush, and aren't there plenty of English settlers around to be tempted?" Then they began to argue again.

September, 1830

Jack Donahoe is Dead ~ Killed on this my Thirteenth Birthday. It happened somewhere on the Bringelly Road. Mr O'Farrell brought us the news. And oh, what a Romantic End! When the troopers challenged the Gang, Jack Donahoe waved his hat Three times in the air, then threw it away and shouted, "Come on. We're ready even if there's a Dozen of you!" Whereupon a Battle broke out. One of the Troopers shot Jack Donahoe through the Heart and the other bushrangers, Webber and Walmesley, turned tail like Rabbits and ran away.

It's hard to believe that the Daring Outlaw we have all talked and thought about for so long, lies Dead at the Age of Twenty-Four ~ only eleven years older than Myself.

"Good riddance to Bad Rubbish," said Ma, but Pa was not so harsh. And I liked the words he said. "Sure and wouldn't any Irishman rather die in Battle than be hung on a Gallows Tree by English soldiers." "Will people always remember him, Pa?" I asked. "I doubt it Lass," he said. "He'll be forgotten in a year or so."

I'm glad I've kept this Diary. At least now I'll be sure to remember the Wild Colonial Boy and perhaps my children may too.

Written by Pat Edwards

JESSE JAMES

Hero or Villain?

Have you seen films about the Wild West
where the gang of bank robbers comes riding
into town? There have been films about
fictitious robbers and about real ones too, such
as Butch Cassidy and the Sundance Kid, Billy
the Kid and Jesse James. There have been over
25 films made about Jesse James, which shows
that he has been a popular figure. In most of
the films these robbers are presented as heroes,
even though they are on the wrong side of the
law. But how true a picture is this? What was
Jesse James really like?

Jesse James was probably the most famous outlaw in the Wild West. Jesse grew up leading a life of crime. He rode with a gang who carried out dangerous and exciting raids, so perhaps it was during this time that Jesse developed a taste for adventure and no respect for the law.

By the time he was nineteen, Jesse was already an outlaw. He was the leader of a gang that included his brother Frank and his relatives the Younger brothers — James, Cole and Bob. Another member of the gang was Robert Ford. Over the years this gang stole thousands of dollars from banks and railways. Large rewards were offered to anyone who could capture them.

Minnesota Daily News

SEPTEMBER 8th 1876

CITIZENS OF NORTHFIELD FIGHT BACK!

YESTERDAY THE NOTORIOUS JESSE JAMES AND HIS GANG WERE SHOWN HOW THE DECENT FOLK OF NORTHFIELD COULD FIGHT BACK.

Jesse has been raiding banks for ten years now and he has been getting away with it. He attempted to raid a bank at Northfield but the citizens put up a fight and drove Jesse's gang out of town. Two members of the gang were killed and several were wounded in a fierce shoot-out.

Jesse was worried. He had to make an escape. He rode out of town, forgetting to cut the telegraph wires. Northfield sent word of the robbery. The people of Minnesota have decided that enough is enough and together they have decided to search for the James gang. Jesse must be brought to justice.

YOUNGER BROTHERS CAPTURED

Members of the Jesse James gang James, Cole and Bob Younger were captured today.

Jesse and Frank were not captured though. They laid low for a little while, but then formed a new gang. Jesse was the most wanted man in the West.

Many people had tried to capture Jesse but had failed. In the end Jesse was caught by someone who knew him — Robert Ford, a member of the old gang.

REWARD!
- DEAD OR ALIVE -

$5,000.00 will be paid for the capture of the men who robbed the bank at

NORTHFIELD, MINN.

They are believed to be Jesse James and his Band, or the Youngers.

All officers are warned to use precaution in making arrest. These are the most desperate men in America.

Take no chances! Shoot to kill!!

J. H. McDonald,
SHERIFF

Robert (Bob) Ford and his brother Charley went to see Jesse at his home. It was 9 o'clock in the morning of April 3rd 1882. The story is that the three men were talking. Jesse stood on a chair to straighten a picture on the wall. Bob Ford drew his gun and shot Jesse in the back.

On Jesse's gravestone the words *Shot by a Coward* were written. Bob Ford, who was on the side of the law when he shot Jesse, was thought of as a villain. Jesse James, leader of a gang responsible for robbing banks and shooting people, was thought of as a kind of hero. Strange isn't it?

And Jesse's brother Frank?
Frank gave himself up and was cheered by the crowds. He had a trial at court — it would have looked like the one in the photograph — but he was acquitted, which means that the charges were dropped. That doesn't seem fair, does it?

69

Gold Fever!

Bandit or bushranger, highwayman or pirate—all asked for, fought for, died for ... GOLD!

And so did ordinary, usually law-abiding citizens during the times of the gold rushes.

What is it about this yellow metal that gives it such power over people?

Why is gold prized so highly?

People who study history believe that gold was probably the first metal to become widely known. And although mining for flint to make weapons and tools would have come first, gold mining would have been close behind. Early people, finding an attractive coloured stone in river and creek beds, turned it into ornaments and jewellery. They liked its colour and its weight. The fact that there was not too much of it around made it more valuable. Before long, they were trading it for goods and property. The more gold you had, the more you could buy—and the richer you became.

When Spanish galleons, laden with gold plundered from the Incas of Peru and the Aztecs of Mexico, set sail from Nombre de Dios, pirate ships gathered like bees to a honey pot. And when exaggerated stories were told of how gold was just lying around waiting to be picked up in California or Australia or New Zealand or the Canadian Yukon, people flocked to these places in their thousands. Along with all the hopeful adventurers were the outlaws and bushrangers who, just like the pirates, were after quick riches. There are lots of romantic tales and songs about these characters, but they were really only common criminals.

Gold is still valued highly. You'll hear it mentioned in the news most nights. But nowadays, people use money, cheques or plastic cards! And we still have outlaws gambling their lives on the chance of easy money. They are called bank robbers and nobody thinks they're romantic!

Who Invented Money?

The answer is no one—and everyone.

But the first money was nothing like the money we use now. You see, anything that people value can be—and is—used for money. For a long, long time in the world's history, men and women simply swapped goods (or "bartered", as it is called). You dealt with a neighbour or went to a market with what you had, in the hope that you could trade it for something else. If you were a tailor you might make a coat in return for a sack of grain. The more things you could get for what you had, the more valuable it was. A Greek warrior's shield, for instance was said to be worth one hundred cattle.

In time, some goods were valued more than others and they became the first money. But it all depended on where you lived. If you were an Aztec Indian, you would have used cocoa beans when you wanted to buy a new shawl or rug. But if you had lived in some parts of Africa you might have used cubes of salt or squares of cloth at the market.

72

In different parts of the world people were busy "spending" copper bracelets, pieces of coral, sea shells, scraps of fur, pieces of leather, nails, rice, even bitter almonds!

The precious metals—gold and silver—were of course the most valuable. But poor people never saw these. You would not have used a lump of gold to buy a loaf of bread or a pair of shoes. For that you needed more common "money"—dried fish if you were an Icelander.

Who invented coins?

It's believed they were invented by the Greeks and by the Chinese around 700 BC. The first state made coins appeared in the kingdom of Lydia in western Asia around 650 BC. They were made of electrum, a mixture of gold and silver which occurs naturally.

73

The first Greek coins came about because Greeks used nuggets of gold and silver when trading. There were crooks even then and it didn't take villains long to come up with the bright idea of covering a lump of metal with gold leaf. Suspicious traders began punching a hole out of each nugget to see if it were truly made of gold. Soon the small round pieces from the centre were being used because they were much handier than the nuggets. The next step was to put a mark on the golden piece—and hey presto!—coins were invented.

In time, every country had its own kind of money, but generally they all used gold and silver for their really valuable coins, and copper (which was cheaper because it was easier to find) for the small coins the poor people used. Coins were easier to carry than fat chickens, they weren't as smelly as dried fish or as fragile as sea shells. Now sellers could set the price of their goods in coins and buyers could be given change. The only trouble was nobody ever had enough money!

74

Paper money was invented by the Chinese around AD 800 and was used until the mid-1400s. Then they went back to copper coins and rice. They still had gold and silver, but these were shaped into small ingots or bars, and only the rich had them.

Bank notes appeared in Sweden in 1661 and in England in 1694, but of course people had been writing notes promising to pay certain amounts ever since they learnt to write. In Venice, traders had been swapping notes since the 1400s. In Britain, in 1709, the Bank of England was given the sole right to issue notes which were used as money throughout the country.

Although Australia was an English colony, the most popular money used there in the early years was Spanish dollars. Governor Macquarie punched holes in these so the coins couldn't be taken away and used in other countries. This also helped solve the problem of scarcity — by punching a hole in a coin, one coin was turned into two, and the supply of money was doubled!

Everyone immediately began calling it the Holey Dollar.

The name "dollar" comes from the German word *Thaler* and that came from the town Joachimsthal in Czechoslovakia. Coins made from metal mined in this town were called *Joachimsthalers*. People shortened that to *thalers* or *dalers* and in time this became "dollar"!

75

The Great Tractor Rescue

*Stories about children driving
powerful and dangerous machines
have always been favourites.
A tractor may seem humble
compared with some machines,
but it is dangerous for children
to try to drive one.
So, wait until you are grown up,
and meanwhile — enjoy this story.*

THERE was once a pair of boys called Teddy and
Gerard who lived in a long secret valley. Wherever
they looked there were hills, dark spiky pine trees, and
bright streams filled with eels and watercress. It was
just the sort of valley for boys to enjoy themselves in.
Each weekday they went to school, but Saturday and
Sunday were all their own, and they wandered all over
the valley visiting both friends and friendly places.

One of their friends was a very strange old woman
indeed. Her name was Mrs Estelle Tadworthy and she
had a son who was a bank manager and lived the
respectable life. Mrs Estelle Tadworthy, however, was
not respectable. Everyone called her Mrs Weeds,
because every weekend she left her house in the town
and came out to the country to collect plants. Not
garden plants either, for she scorned those. She chose
the wild and weedy ones. She did not ever call them
weeds, however, but always referred to them as
"herbs". Most people thought Mrs Weeds was a little
mad and she did look rather unusual wearing curious
brown smocks which she wove and dyed herself, and
funny old sandals tied up with string. She wouldn't

76

wear a hat at all. Her long grey hair either tossed and tangled around her brown face or stuck out in two tight little plaits with green ribbons on the end. Rain or shine she always carried a stout green umbrella. It didn't worry her when people said she was crazy.

"Because I'm brown doesn't mean I'm dirty," she would say. "Because I don't do the same as every other fool, but like my own foolishness best, doesn't mean to say I'm crazy. Some like me, some don't," said Mrs Weeds. "That's how it is . . ."

Teddy and Gerard were two who liked her a lot. They liked her thin bony face and long gentle hands. They liked the way she roared with laughter at her own jokes, the way she wore purple clover flowers behind her ears and the way she talked to plants and trees as she went along the road. She gave the boys all sorts of leaves to eat, telling them how good they would be for them.

77

"This is sorrel and this is dandelion," she said. "Eat them both to help keep your livers clean." The boys found the dandelion leaves hot to taste, but they liked the tangy flavour of the sorrel. Mrs Weeds said her liver was extremely clean and that was why she never got headaches or grumpy feelings. "It's the dandelion and sorrel that does it," she said.

One Saturday, just before Christmas, when the foxgloves were out, ringing white and purple bells on every hillside in the valley, and when the streams and boggy bits were green and yellow with watercress and kingcups, Teddy and Gerard went crawling behind a hedge pretending to escape from enemies. There was a rich earthy smell because the farmer who owned the field was ploughing it up to plant turnips. In fact, the boys went past his tractor standing alone by the gate where he had left it to go home for lunch.

"Anyhow, I could drive that tractor," said Teddy.

"So could I," said Gerard, "but we haven't got time now — our enemies will catch us if we wait to try out a tractor." They went crawling on. Then suddenly they heard a voice coming down the road. It was their friend Mrs Weeds talking aloud to a particularly fine foxglove.

"Hello, you fellow in your purple coat!" she shouted "It's a lovely day. Why are you leaning over like that? Do you want to see who's going by or are your roots weak?"

"Shall we jump out and frighten Mrs Weeds?" asked Teddy in a whisper. Gerard thought perhaps Mrs Weeds would not like *that* at all, but while he was thinking this, someone else sprang out at Mrs Weeds from the other side of the road. Two tremendous tall fellows with guns and rope leaped out of the foxgloves and shouted.

"Hands up, Mrs Estelle Tadworthy!" (Which was
Mrs Weeds' real name, you'll remember.) Mrs Weeds
stopped and peered at them.

"You have the bleary-eyed look that shows a lack of
Vitamin A. The humble carrot would help you a lot,"
she said sharply. "And who might you be?" It was plain,
however, that they were wicked robbers or some such.

"We are thieves and bandits," said the uglier of the
two men, pointing his gun at her. "I am the thief and
he is the bandit. We are going to kidnap you and never
ever let you go until your rich son, Mr John
Tadworthy, prominent businessman and bank
manager that he is, pays us £1,000 sterling."

"I'll pound you and I'll sterling your friend," Mrs
Weeds replied, taking her umbrella in a firm grip.
"The first one that comes near me shall taste the power
of my strong right arm."

Which shows that, though people said Mrs Weeds was slightly mad, she was actually very sensible and brave as a lion. Gerard could see, however, that even brown strong Mrs Weeds couldn't fight two kidnappers with guns and a long snaky rope. Fortunately he had a plan. He whispered it to Teddy, and Teddy understood at once though it was very hard to hear, what with the defiant screams of Mrs Weeds and the yells of the robbers, who were being hit with the umbrella.

Gerard's plan was this — that Teddy should drive the farmer's tractor down the road to rescue Mrs Weeds. In the meantime, he, Gerard, the best runner in the school, would try to lead at least one of the kidnappers away so that there would be only one left for Mrs Weeds and Teddy to deal with. Once round the corner Gerard would climb up a certain tree, and it would be Teddy's job to drive the tractor and Mrs Weeds underneath that tree so that Gerard could drop down onto it from the branches like a monkey or Tarzan in the pictures. This way, said Gerard, they would have an exciting adventure and be helpful to Mrs Weeds as well.

Teddy could scarcely get at the tractor quickly enough. He made off, hidden by the hedge while Gerard crouched in the soft ploughed earth watching the battle that raged in the road. Mrs Weeds was fighting magnificently, but she was getting a bit tired. You could not expect an old woman to fight both a thief and a bandit even if she was a fine muscular old woman with a remarkably clean liver.

Teddy went straight to the farmer's tractor. Quick as a flash he tried the knobs and levers and found how to start it immediately. He steered it round and out through the gateway forgetting, in his hurry, to open the gate. Fortunately, its hinges were rusty and old and snapped easily, so Teddy was very soon grinding

down the road, with the tractor in top gear, off to
rescue Mrs Weeds. The only troublesome thing was the
gate which was stuck across the front of the tractor.

Now when Gerard heard the tractor grating along
the road and knew Teddy was coming, he wriggled out
under the hedge and shouted, "Leave Mrs Weeds
alone!" He charged fiercely at the thief.

The thief was just about to pop a loop of rope over
Mrs Weeds' head when Gerard butted him squarely in
the stomach. "Oof!" said the thief and sat down hard
on the road.

"I'm off to get the police," Gerard said. "I shall tell
them who you are, and describe your pasty faces to the
last miserable whisker."

Naturally the kidnappers could not allow that.

"You look after the old woman and I'll catch the
boy. We'll kidnap them both," yelled the bandit, and
set off after Gerard leaving the thief to struggle with
Mrs Weeds. You could see the bandit did not know that
Gerard was a splendid runner — the fastest in the school.

At this moment Teddy drove the tractor into sight, steering it straight for Mrs Weeds and the thief.

"Jump on, Mrs Weeds," he called. "Jump on!" And, looking up and seeing what was coming and who was driving it, Mrs Weeds thrust her knobbly right fist at the thief, in a fine upper-cut, and scooping up her umbrella from the road, skilfully ducked round the gate (which still hung in front of the tractor), and nipped up beside Teddy. The thief was rather dazed. First he had been butted by Gerard and then boxed by Mrs Weeds. But worse was in store for him. He was too bewildered to notice the gate. As he went to leap after Mrs Weeds he hit the gate and lay flattened and dusty while the tractor ground on its way.

"I shall hit his fingers with my umbrella if he tries to climb after us," said Mrs Weeds, but the thief just lay in the dust and let them go on, steadily but not very fast.

They went round the corner. There was the tree with the bandit standing underneath it, looking into the branches that reached out over the road. There among the leaves crouched Gerard, like a monkey boy. The bandit who did not like climbing trees was trying to poke him down with a stick. He stopped and peered through his horn-rimmed glasses in astonishment. He dodged out of the way of the sticking-out gate and tried to scramble onto the tractor to get at Teddy and Mrs Weeds. Mrs Weeds was waiting with her umbrella and he had to let go again. As the tractor passed under the tree Gerard swung down from the branches onto it.

Off they went, leaving the bandit and the thief behind.

Mrs Weeds roared with delighted laughter, startling a bull in a nearby paddock.

"You're a fine couple of fellows," she said. "More than a match for any kidnappers. Usually I like a bit of a scrap, but I was getting out of breath, I must admit." She slapped them on their backs. Teddy and Gerard looked proudly at each other out of the corners of their eyes. They grinned at Mrs Weeds. The tractor went rumble rumble bumble along the road. All seemed happy.

But . . . just at that moment a car roared up behind them and sitting at the wheel, his eyes narrow and fierce behind his glasses, was the bandit, while at his side, looking bruised and angry, sat the thief.

"Of course! They would have a car hidden!" cried Teddy in despair, for the car went much faster than the tractor. "What shall we do?"

Then Mrs Weeds climbed up onto the engine of the tractor and unscrewed the petrol cap. From the wide pockets of her smock she took dandelions, sorrel, yarrow, forgetmenots, wild parsley and mint, clover, nettles and all sorts of plants, jammed them into the tank and then screwed the cap on again. Teddy, looking over his shoulder, saw the thief leaning out of the car window and trying to lassoo the tractor with

the rope he had been using earlier for tying up Mrs
Weeds. But at that moment the tractor gave a roar like
a bull and leaped forward at the speed of an express
railway train. It was plain that Mrs Weeds' plants had
mingled with the petrol in some mysterious way to
make a powerful mixture that the tractor loved. Teddy
steered, Gerard worked the gears, and Mrs Weeds
stood, tall and brown, with her grey hair blowing out
like a flag in the wind they made by going so fast.

"We've left them miles behind," said Gerard,
turning round. But no! There behind them bumping
and bowling along was the kidnappers' car, and the
bandit and thief were crouched inside it white as
unpleasant cheese, and obviously terrified. The lassoo
the thief had thrown had first caught the tractor and
then whipped itself into a knot round the car's
bumper. Neither the bandit nor the thief could get out
of the car and the car could not get free of the tractor,
so they sped wildly along together, on and on up hill
and down until they came in sight of the nearest town.
The tractor dashed into the main street, and then
suddenly, without warning, it slowed down, and it
stopped right in front of the police station.

A policeman with a ginger moustache was standing
outside. He looked first at the tractor and then peered
into the car.

"My word!" he shouted. "Here are those wicked criminals — the bandit and the thief. Catch them, catch them!" He blew on his whistle and policemen of all shapes and sizes came running from everywhere, seized the white-faced and trembling bandit, the battered and bruised thief and hurried them into prison, which was where they belonged.

So that was the end of the great tractor rescue in which Teddy and Gerard rescued their friend Mrs Weeds from kidnappers. But it was not quite the end because next weekend, Mrs Weeds came out to visit them and brought with her boxes of delightful seeds with instructions on how to grow them. They dug and planted (and Mrs Weeds dug and planted with them) and then they waited — and sure enough, two weeks later up came sage, up came parsley, marjoram, thyme, sweet basil, summer savory, dill, and all the nice garden herbs (pot herbs, as some call them) that give good rich tastes and smells to cooking. The boys' mother was delighted and the boys themselves were proud to have such good herb gardens, and looked after them carefully.

As for Mrs Weeds, she went on roaming the countryside, and when the story of the great tractor rescue got round, no kidnapper ever dared approach her as she strode on her way, her hair blowing grey and wild around her, her stout green umbrella under her arm, talking to trees and flowers as if they were the best of friends, as indeed they were.

Written by Margaret Mahy
illustrated by Liz Roberts

**Outlaws can be outwitted by using your head!
See if you can solve . . .**

The Case of the
Kidnapped Brain

Amy Adams and "Hawkeye" Collins are two young super sleuths who watch over the citizens of Lakewood Hills. They are both aged 12 and they are in 6th grade at the local primary school.

Sergeant Treadwell of the Lakewood Hills Police Department says: "I don't know what Lakewood Hills ever did without Amy and Hawkeye — they've cracked so many tough cases. Whenever I have a problem I can't solve, I know just where to go — straight to these two super sleuths."

When Lakewood Hills Primary School's own resident genius, Newton Pestle, is kidnapped, Sergeant Treadwell calls in Amy and Hawkeye to help him solve "The Case of the Kidnapped Brain". Why Newton? Did the kidnappers want to force the young computer expert to help them commit an undetectable crime — or was there something more sinister behind his disappearance? Even Amy and Hawkeye are stumped until Newton himself manages to give them the vital clue.

How did Amy discover that the ransom note was really a coded message? There's a clue somewhere. Can you spot it, too? When you've "cracked the case" or even if you're not quite sure — turn to page 94 and read the secret mirror-writing to solve the mystery.

The tension in the air at Lakewood Hills Primary School almost crackled. The halls, the classrooms and the cafeteria all buzzed with the news: Newton Pestle had been kidnapped.

Again and again, a question arose in hushed, worried conversations among teachers and students — why Newton?

Sure, Newton was a genius; he went to Lakewood Hills Primary only to learn how to get along with kids. During IQ testing at the school, a special team had been brought in from the nearby State Institute of Learning Research specifically to watch him and talk with him. Newton had quite simply blown them away. The team had no scale that could measure his intelligence.

When he was a fourth-grader, Newton designed and built a computer that beat the International Chess Federation's computer in a series of one hundred chess games — with no losses. Then Newton played against his own invention and beat it thirty-three times in a row. During the thirty-fourth game, the computer burst into flames. Newton got up from his chair and walked away, muttering, "Check and mate".

Still, kidnapping a sixth-grader who was a genius and built computers didn't make sense. Newton, an only child, lived with his parents in a pleasant little house on Maple Street, south of the Lakedale Shopping Mall. His mother worked part-time at the public library, and his father was a salesman for an office-supplies company and travelled frequently in his work. The Pestle family was comfortable, but far from wealthy. A kidnapper just wouldn't pick Newton as a victim if he wanted a lot of ransom money.

Hawkeye Collins and Amy Adams sat with the rest of the sixth-grade class. Their eyes locked on the front of the room as Officer Ellis of the Lakewood Hills Police Department walked in and handed a folded note to Mr Bronson, their teacher. Mr Bronson read the note, nodded to Officer Ellis, and cleared his throat.

"Amy and Hawkeye, please go along with Officer Ellis. This has been cleared with your parents. If you want to, you may call home from the principal's office before you leave."

Both Hawkeye and Amy got up from their desks.

"That's okay, Mr Bronson," Hawkeye said. "We're ready to go, right, Amy?"

Amy nodded. "Right. We don't need to call anyone, Mr Bronson."

Officer Ellis drove the police car a bit faster than normal between the school and police headquarters — a distance of a few short blocks. Both sixth-graders noticed that Officer Ellis had unsnapped the security strap that held her service revolver in its holster.

"What's this all —" Amy began.

"Sorry," the officer interrupted. "No questions and no conversation. Sergeant Treadwell will fill you in at his office."

Hawkeye and Amy exchanged nervous, confused looks. "Wow!" Hawkeye mouthed silently. Amy fidgeted uneasily, nibbling on her lower lip.

Sergeant Treadwell looked both grim and official as he sat behind his strangely clutter-free desk. A middle-aged, athletic-looking man in a grey business suit stood next to Sarge, holding a large manila envelope.

"Amy, Hawkeye," Sarge said, "this gentleman is Investigator Michael Auborn of the National Security Council. He asked that you two be brought in on this case even before I suggested it."

"National Security? Case? What case, Sarge?" asked a bewildered Hawkeye.

"The kidnapping of Newton Pestle," Investigator Auborn answered. "Please keep in mind that anything — and everything — we discuss in this office today is essential to the security of our country. Nothing is to go beyond these walls — *ever*. Is that completely understood?"

"Yes, sir," Amy and Hawkeye answered together.

"Okay. Good. We — the Security Council — have heard about you two youngsters. You do excellent work. We're proud of you." Investigator Auborn allowed himself a brief smile.

"Now on to business. Frank Pestle, Newton's father, is an undercover agent for the federal government. Some — individuals — must have broken his cover. We assume they've kidnapped his son to force Mr Pestle to give them certain information.

"We don't think Newton has been harmed — yet. We have to find him very quickly, but we have next to nothing to go on. Mr Pestle found a tape of Newton's voice in his mailbox. It's a common brand of tape, available almost anywhere. There were no fingerprints. The voice on the tape is Newton's; we've verified that through voiceprints we have on record of all our people and their families. Sergeant Treadwell believes the tape can tell you far more than it's told us. That's why we've called you in to help us."

Sarge took a small cassette player from his drawer and placed it in the centre of his desk. He also handed a sheet of paper to Amy and Hawkeye.

"I'll play the tape," he said, "and you can follow the words on the paper. You *know* Newton — we don't. If you're as clever now as you have been before, you may find the lead — the key — we're all missing."

"Sarge," Amy protested, "Newton's always been a loner. We don't really know him — at least, not in the way you seem to think we do. I don't think we —"

Sarge held up his hand. "We realise that, Amy. But you and Hawkeye have been in the same grade and class with Newton for six years — seven, counting kindergarten. That puts you way ahead of us. There's an answer in this tape. There *has* to be. A youngster as bright as Newton wouldn't just jabber if he had a chance to let us know where he is. Maybe — just maybe — you'll be able to dig out what he's saying. All we can ask is that you do your best. Okay?"

"Of course we'll do our best, Sarge," Hawkeye said.

"Yeah," added Amy, "but we sure hope our best is good enough. Whether we understand him or not, Newton is still our friend."

Sarge pushed a button on the tape player, and Newton's voice filled the office.

"Officer Larson: Drop money in Loon Lake, or leave dough Monday in leakproof lockboxes. Only listen; don't make idiotic, lousy I —"

"That's enough, you twerp!" a rough male voice cut in suddenly. The tape played out silently to its end.

Hawkeye shook his head, as if in shock.

"I don't believe it! He didn't say *where* in Loon Lake, or whether the money in the lockboxes is to go in the lake, or even how much money — hey, I thought you said this wasn't a money case anyway! What gives?"

Amy's voice was shaky. "And who's Officer Larson? There's nobody on the force with that name. I'm afraid he's drugged," she said. "He must be. Newton never would've said 'dough', either."

"No, Amy," Investigator Auborn said. "Our voice analysis equipment shows no sign of any type of drug. Newton was definitely all right when he made this tape."

Hawkeye began pacing about the office.

Amy held the typed transcript, studying it. "He's leaving out words, too — twice he forgot the word *the*. It almost sounds like a coded message . . . hmm . . . but it looks too random. There's no sequence."

"How about dropping every other word, or every third word — something like that?" Hawkeye suggested.

"No . . . no, . . ." Amy murmured, deep in thought. "Newton seemed to be speaking just the slightest bit more slowly than he usually does . . . as if he were calculating, planning each letter or word, rather than . . . just . . . just — Hey! Sarge, I think I've got something! Look at this transcript! I think we may have found our kidnapped genius–thanks to the genius himself!"

LAKEWOOD HILLS POLICE DEPARTMENT
150 WEST STREET   LAKEWOOD HILLS   55331

OFFICIAL TRANSCRIPT

Date recorded   8 March 1988
Date transcribed   8 March 1988
Message taken by   Officer ELLIS

TEXT:

<u>Boy's voice</u>: "Officer Larson, Drop money in Loon Lake, or leave dough Monday in leakproof lockboxes. Only listen; don't make idiotic, lousy l. . ."

<u>Man's voice</u>, interrupting: "That's enough, you twerp."

Sound of movement, then tape goes blank for rest of cassette.

I hereby certify that the foregoing text is a faithful transcription of the conversation in question.

Officer's Signature _Louise Ellis_ ..... Date 8ᵗʰ March 88

The Case of the
Kidnapped   Brain

Hold this page up to a mirror and you'll be able to read the solution for yourself.

Amy saw through Newton's strange message by reading only the first letter of each word, which yielded the message, "OLD MILL OLD MILL OLD MILL –" before Newton was stopped.

"It just seemed like such a dumb message from Newton," she explained. "I knew he was saying more than it seemed".

The police went to the old mill near Lakewood Hills and forced the kidnappers to give up Newton without any violence. The gang members were convicted of kidnapping and sentenced to prison.

Since Mr Pestle's cover was blown, he could no longer function as an undercover agent. He could, however, function very well as chief of detectives and special investigator for the Lakewood Hills Police Department. And his work gave him far more time with his wife and his very special son, Newton.

Glossary

alias *(p. 22)*
also known as

assigned *(p. 31)*
sent to work

booty *(p. 22)*
stolen goods

bushrangers *(p. 44)*
criminals who
lived as outlaws in
the bush in
Australia

cutlass *(p. 16)*
a short sword
which is slightly
curved

dirk *(p. 21)*
dagger

doubloon *(p. 17)*
old Spanish gold
coin

fictitious *(p. 66)*
imagined;
invented

foggity foul *(p. 27)*
a poetical way of
describing how
dirty the pirate
ship was

fragile *(p. 74)*
easily broken

hatchet *(p. 25)*
a short axe

hold *(p. 20)*
the part of a ship
below deck where
the cargo is stored

**internal combustion
engine** *(p. 60)*
modern car
engines are an
example

isthmus *(p. 20)*
a narrow strip of
land connecting
two larger areas of
land

lenient *(p. 24)*
gentle; merciful

Glossary continues on
page 96

Glossary

Lincoln green (*p. 45*)
  a bright green cloth once made at Lincoln in England

lummox (*p. 11*)
  clumsy, stupid person

manila envelope (*p. 90*)
  envelope made out of strong, brown paper

mutinied (*p. 22*)
  rebelled against those in charge

notorious (*p. 30*)
  well-known for some bad quality

pedigree (*p. 27*)
  pure-bred

piece of eight (*p. 17*)
  old Spanish coin

plundered (*p. 21*)
  took things by force

prey on (*p. 21*)
  hunt

promptly (*p. 26*)
  quickly

rollicking rip (*p. 27*)
  someone who behaves in a rough noisy way

scarcity (*p.75*)
  inadequate supply

scorned (*p. 76*)
  rejected

scuttled (*p. 28*)
  sunk

sinister (*p. 88*)
  evil

sleuth (*p. 88*)
  detective

smuggle (*p. 14*)
  bring something into a country secretly without paying the customs duties

strait (*p. 18*)
  narrow stretch of water separating two areas of land

swaggering gait (*p. 27*)
  walk that shows how important you feel

tickly tarry line (*p.27*)
  a poetical way of describing the hangman's rope

turnpike gates (*p.54*)
  gates where you pay some money in order to be able to use the road

verified (*p.90*)
  checked that it was true

yellow-boys (*p.58*)
  gold coins